SKELETON
MEETS THE MUMMY

by Steve Metzger
illustrated by Aaron Zenz

SCHOLASTIC INC.

New York Toronto London Auckland
Sydney Mexico City New Delhi Hong Kong

To Jenne Abramowitz
—S.M.

For Granny—Bess Hankinson
—A.Z.

ISBN 978-0-545-23032-2

12 11 10 9 8 7 6 5 4 3 2   10 11 12 13 14 15/0

Printed in the U.S.A.   40

First printing, September 2010

Book design by Aaron Zenz and Jennifer Rinaldi Windau

Sammy couldn't wait to go trick-or-treating.

He didn't even need a costume.

"Not so fast!" his mother called. Sammy stopped with a click and a clack. "I need you to bring this thermos of hot soup to Grandma Bones. There's a chill in the air tonight."

"But, Mom!" Sammy said. "Derek is waiting for me."
"It's just a short walk through the woods," said his
mother. "You'll still have plenty of time to get candy
with your friend."

"OK," Sammy said. He took the soup and stepped out into the Halloween night.

It's kind of dark, Sammy thought as he slowly walked through the woods.

Flap!

Something flew past Sammy's head. *Oh, it's only a bat*, he thought.

Whoosh! Swoosh!

Sammy froze with a shake and a rattle. *Oh, it's only the wind*, he thought.

Sammy saw a monster!
Oh, it's only a tree, he thought.

Scritch! Scratch!

Sammy heard the crunching of leaves.

Something was following him.

Sammy walked faster.

Scritch! Scratch!

It was right behind him.

What is it? Sammy wondered.

He was afraid to look.

Sammy started to run.

Scritch! Scratch!

It was still right behind him.

Sammy looked back and saw . . .

. . . a MUMMY!

Click! Clack!

Sammy ran as fast as he could.

But the mummy ran fast, too.

Scritch! Scratch!

The mummy was getting closer . . .

. . . and closer . . .

. . . and closer!

Huff! Puff! Huff! Puff!

Sammy was tired of running. Sammy was tired of being afraid.

Flippety flap!

Flippety flap!

Sammy heard a flapping sound coming from the mummy. And then he had an idea.

Sammy turned around, grabbed a loose piece of cloth, and pulled with all his might.

He pulled and pulled and pulled. The mummy spun and spun and spun.

Sammy couldn't believe it! The mummy wasn't a mummy at all! It was . . .

. . . his friend Derek!

"You scared me!" Sammy exclaimed.

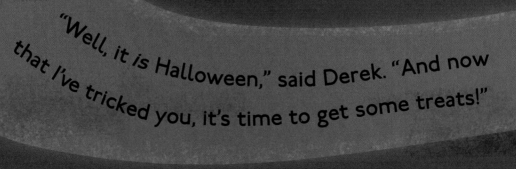

"Well, it is Halloween," said Derek. "And now that I've tricked you, it's time to get some treats!"

"OK!" Sammy said. "But before we start,
I have to go see my grandmother."

"Don't you mean your grand*mummy*?" Derek joked.

"Yeah," said Sammy. "Race you there!"